BLAZE AND THE MONSTER MACHINES: AN ICY RESCUE
A CENTUM BOOK 9781910917091

Published in Great Britain by Centum Books Ltd

This edition published 2016
© 2016 Viacom International Inc. All Rights Reserved.

1 3 5 7 9 10 8 6 4 2

Centum Books Ltd, 20 Devon Square, Newton Abbot, Devon, TQ12 2HR, UK
books@centumbooksltd.co.uk

CENTUM BOOKS Limited Reg. No. 07641486

A CIP catalogue record for this book is available from the British Library.

Printed in China.

Blaze, AJ and Gabby are zooming through the forest.
It's one of their favourite places to drive.

READY TO ROLL!

There's a jump up ahead.

"Hey Blaze, see if you can do a flip!" says Gabby.

Blaze speeds towards the ramp …

… jumps into the air …

… and does an awesome flip!

WAA-HOOOO!

4

They skid to a stop.
"Nice one, Blaze!
A perfect landing," says Gabby.

"Yeah, that was ah … ah …"

"AH-CHOOO!"

GASKETS! Blaze sneezes, **one ... two ... three** more times.

Gabby the mechanic does a check-up.
"**Stick out your tongue and say 'ahh',**" she says to Blaze.

"Blaze, you've got the **SNEEZLES!**"

The Sneezles is a cold that makes Monster Machines sneeze all the time.

Luckily, Gabby has just what Blaze needs …
MEDICINE OIL.
"Just one sip and your Sneezles will all be gone."

"You did it, Gabby!" says Blaze.
The Medicine Oil has cured Blaze's Sneezles.

Just then, Pickle calls AJ on his wrist computer. "Something very strange is happening. Everyone is sneezing!" says Pickle.

"AH ..."

"AH ..."

Darington, Zeg, Stripes, Starla and Crusher have all got the Sneezles!

Blaze, AJ and Gabby need to get the Medicine Oil to their friends.

"We'd better hurry. We're a long way from the Monster Dome," says AJ.

Blaze races through the forest, swerving trees and jumping over logs.

ZOOOOM!

HUBCAPS!

To get to their friends,
they need to climb up
a huge waterfall.

"But we can't climb up
water, Blaze," says AJ.

Gabby has an idea.
"Maybe we can!"
She checks her thermometer.

If the red line goes down to 0, the
WATER WILL TURN INTO ICE.

That's it! It's so cold that
the waterfall freezes.

Now that the water has turned into ice, they can climb the waterfall!
AJ grabs a climbing hook.

"Let's climb!"

They've made it to the top!
HIGH TYRE!

Meanwhile back at the Monster Dome,
the trucks can't stop sneezing!

"Oh boy!" says Pickle.
"Don't worry. Blaze,
AJ and Gabby are
bringing medicine."

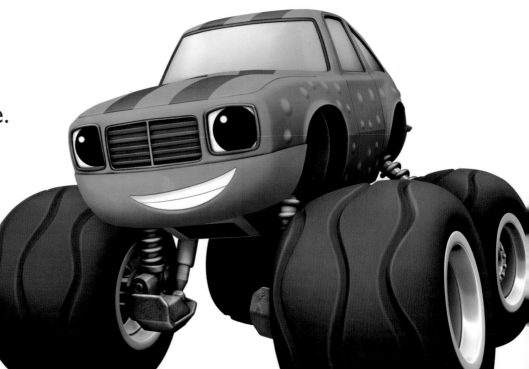

Crusher is baking in the kitchen. He won't admit that he's got the Sneezles!

"What if you sneeze again?" asks Pickle.

"No way. I'm not going to sneeze ah ... ah ..."

"AH-CHOOO!"

Crusher's sneeze is so big that he knocks over his baking bowl. Yuck!

The Monster Machines need help – **FAST!**

Blaze, AJ and Gabby are on their way!
They zip down a snowy mountain, but there's a strange rumble.
"That's weird. It feels like the whole mountain is shaking," says Gabby.

GASKETS! IT'S AN AVALANCHE!

Blaze speeds them away.

They escape into a cave, just in time.
"Phew, that was close!" says Blaze.

"AH-CHOOO!"

AJ hears someone
sneezing … but who
is it this time?

IT'S A PENGUIN TRUCK!

"Aw, poor guy," says Gabby. He has the Sneezles, too. Luckily she has her Medicine Oil to fix him right up!

The penguin truck is so happy to be feeling better. He shows his new friends a tunnel out of the cave.

Gabby hops onto the penguin to ride with him.
"**FOLLOW ME!**" calls Blaze.

Blaze, AJ, Gabby and the penguin fly through the tunnel, slipping and sliding all the way.

UH-OH!
"Big icicles up ahead!"
says AJ.
How will they get past?

They jump over the icicles!
WAA-HOOOO!

With help from the penguin, they make it to the end of the tunnel. Gabby hugs him goodbye.

Just a little further and they'll be at the Monster Dome.

Nothing can stop them now …
except maybe some **BIG HORNS!**

Big Horns love to bump. They chase after
Blaze, bumping and bashing into him.
How will Blaze, AJ and Gabby get away?

Blaze transforms into an ice-making Monster Machine! **"TIME TO GIVE YOU THE SLIP!"**

Blaze drops blocks of ice, and the Big Horns slip all over the place. The friends get away. Way to go, Blaze!

Finally, they can
see the Monster Dome.
Blaze uses his ice maker
to make an ice slide all the
way back.

"Deploying speed boosters,"
says Blaze. The boosters
blast them down the ice and
back to the dome.

BLAZING SPEED!

The Monster Machines are so pleased to see their friends. "Gaskets! You guys have the Sneezles bad." Blaze says. Gabby treats Stripes, Zeg, Darington, Starla and Crusher with her Medicine Oil.

"WOO-HOO,"

cheer the Monster Machines.
NO MORE SNEEZLES!

MEDICINE OIL

Gabby the mechanic helps fix the Sneezles with her **MEDICINE OIL**. When do you take medicine?

Zoom back through the story and **POINT** to the machines that Gabby fixes with Medicine Oil.

TRICKY TROUBLE

Blaze, AJ and Gabby face lots of problems on their way to the Monster Dome. Can you **REMEMBER** what they do?

HOW do they get **UP** the **WATERFALL**?

WHERE do they **HIDE** from the **AVALANCHE**?

HOW do they get **OUT** of the **CAVE**?

Now race back and **FIND** these moments in the story.

When they find themselves in a cave, AJ hears a mystery sneeze. What **NEW FRIEND** has the Sneezles? Peek past the snow for a clue.

Who hugs this wheeled friend? **SPOT** the page in the story.

BIG HORN CHASE

Blaze meets a herd of Big Horn trucks on his adventure. Which woolly animal do the Big Horns look like?

How many Big Horns **BUMP** into Blaze in the story? Flip back and see.

To get past the icicles, Blaze and the gang have to jump **OVER** them. Point to the pictures where they are **OVER** the icicles.

What's the
OPPOSITE
of over?

FREEZING COLD

When does Gabby use her thermometer?
FIND it in the story.

What number does the red line drop to? That's **ZERO DEGREES CELSIUS** – the temperature that water turns into ice!

20
15
10
5
0